THE CINDER-EYED CATS

ERIC ROHMANN

Crown Publishers, Inc., New York

In faraway lands,

When twilight falls on fair and wind-swept days,

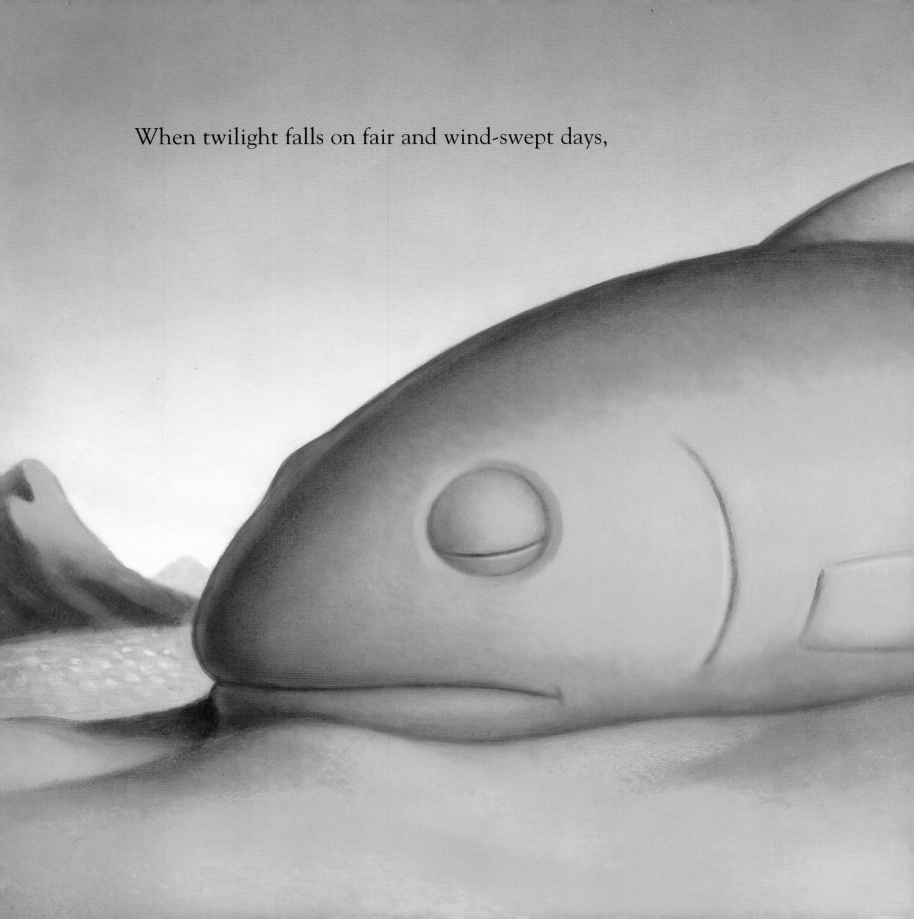

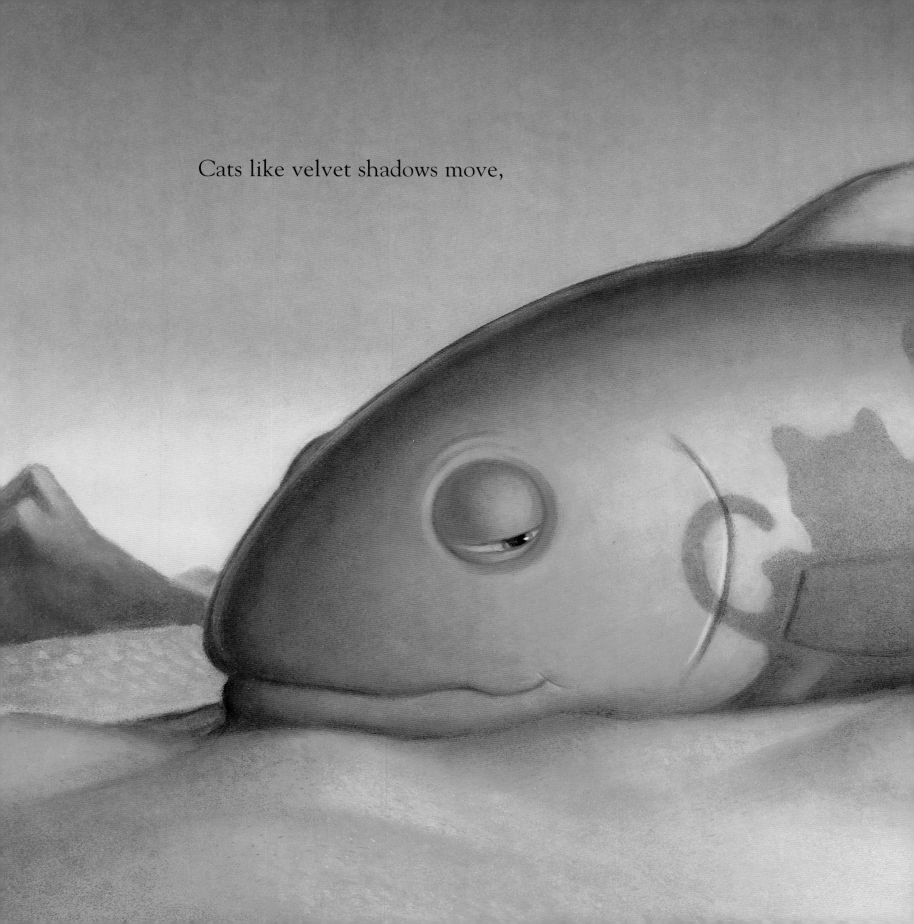

Cats like velvet shadows move,

Their coal-fire eyes ablaze.

And on those bright and moonlit nights while all the world's asleep,

Creatures wake beneath the waves and rise up from the deep.

The moonlight whirls, the stars burst out,
The sand and wind and ocean sway,
And from the grip of earth and sea,
The creatures make their getaway.

Throughout the night the tunas twirl, the starfish weave and wiggle,
And as the sardines dance, their shiny brine-filled bellies jiggle.

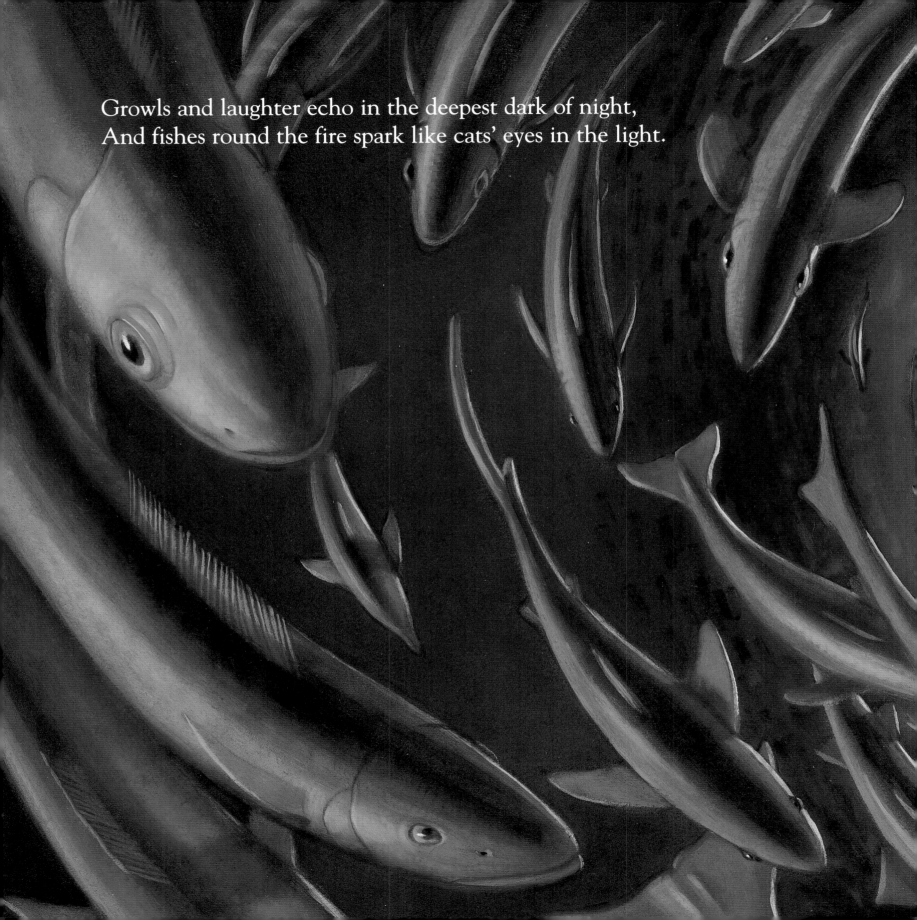

Growls and laughter echo in the deepest dark of night,
And fishes round the fire spark like cats' eyes in the light.

Then a flash of early morning sun, the waking light of dawn,
Calls the creatures to the sea,

And suddenly they're gone.

Quiet now the sea-blue sky, no dancing on the shore—

Until the twilight falls again

And the moon comes round once more.

Published by Crown Publishers, Inc., a Random House company,
201 East 50th Street, New York, New York 10022

CROWN is a trademark of Crown Publishers, Inc.

Printed in Singapore

http://www.randomhouse.com/

Library of Congress Cataloging-in-Publication Data

Rohmann, Eric.
The cinder-eyed cats / Eric Rohmann. — 1st ed.
p. cm.
Summary: A boy makes a magical trip to a tropical island where he and five cinder-eyed
cats watch as various sea creatures emerge from the ocean to dance by their campfire.
[1. Night—Fiction. 2. Marine animals—Fiction. 3. Cats—Fiction. 4. Stories in rhyme.]
I. Title
PZ7.R6413Ci 1997
[E]—dc21
97-6763 CIP

ISBN 0-517-70896-5 (trade)
      0-517-70897-3 (lib. bdg.)

10 9 8 7 6 5 4 3 2 1

First Edition